To my mother
and to my father in memoriam

The Cow Who Wouldn't Come Down

story and pictures by

PAUL BRETT JOHNSON

A TRUMPET CLUB SPECIAL EDITION

Published by The Trumpet Club, Inc.,
a subsidiary of Bantam Doubleday Dell Publishing Group, Inc.,
1540 Broadway, New York, New York 10036.
"A Trumpet Club Special Edition" with the portrayal of a trumpet
and two circles is a registered trademark of
Bantam Doubleday Dell Publishing Group, Inc.

ISBN 0-440-83683-2

This edition reprinted by arrangement with Orchard Books.

Printed in the United States of America
February 1996
10 9 8 7 6 5 4 3 2
UPR

Book design by Mina Greenstein.
The text of this book is set in 16 point Esprit Medium.
The illustrations are acrylic paintings reproduced in full color.

Miss Rosemary knew Gertrude had a mind of her
own. Even so, the day that Gertrude took to flying,
it put Miss Rosemary in something of a tizzy.

"This won't do. It just won't do!" she fussed and
stewed. There was no telling what people would say.
Besides, Miss Rosemary hadn't the slightest notion
how to milk a flying cow.

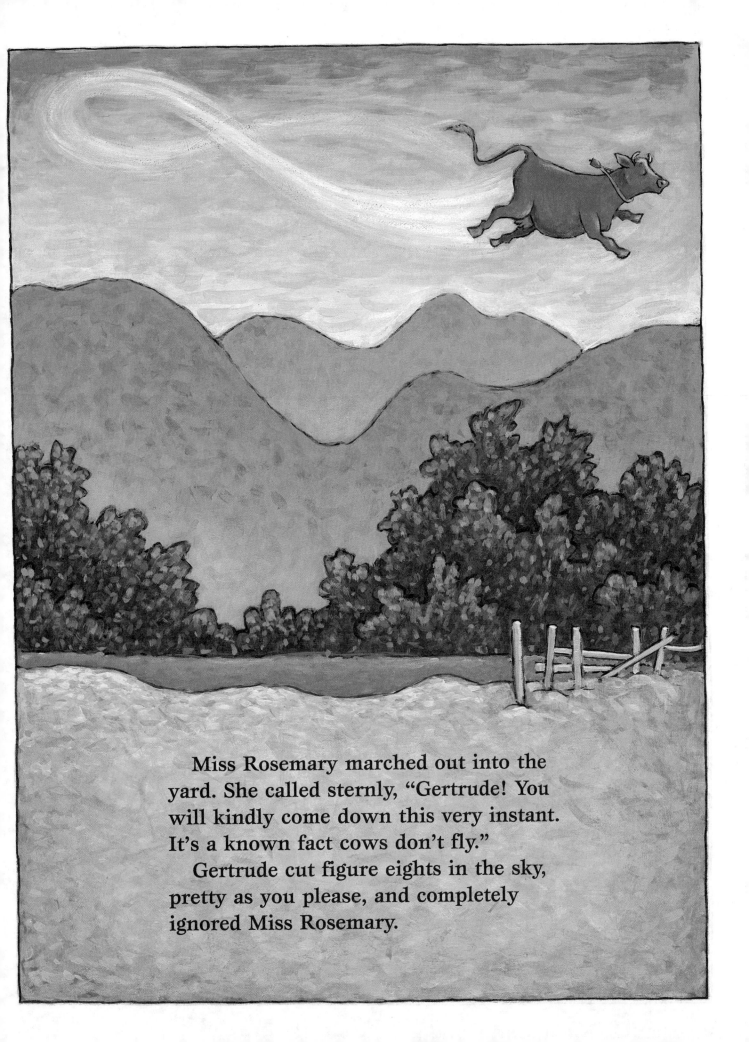

Miss Rosemary marched out into the yard. She called sternly, "Gertrude! You will kindly come down this very instant. It's a known fact cows don't fly."

Gertrude cut figure eights in the sky, pretty as you please, and completely ignored Miss Rosemary.

Miss Rosemary tried again. "Gertrude? Oh, Gerrr-trude. It's time to come down now. Here's a fresh bale of sweet alfalfa. You love alfalfa."

Gertrude took a nose dive, caught an updraft, and sailed into a lazy glide. She did not, however, come down.

Poor Miss Rosemary. It was plain to see she was getting nowhere. She pulled her chin and knitted her brow. Somehow she must bring that silly, contrary cow down.

Miss Rosemary hurried to the shed and sorted through her fishing gear. She chose a sturdy rod and returned to the yard. When Gertrude made an especially low swoop, Miss Rosemary drew back and let go. But her fishing line became tangled in some overhead branches. She missed Gertrude entirely.

Gertrude perched in a tree and tried to sound like a bird. *"Murp, murp."*

"Oh, Gertrude, do hush," Miss Rosemary grumbled. "It's a known fact cows don't murp. They moo."

Miss Rosemary had another idea. She found a long rope, made a lasso, and climbed the attic stairs. She crouched by the window, breathless, and waited.

Finally Gertrude whizzed by, and Miss Rosemary hurled the lasso. All she captured was a nooseful of air. "Gertrude, you are the limit!" she fumed, and stomped her feet.

Miss Rosemary was not about to give up, however. She climbed very cautiously out the window and onto the roof. Inch by inch, she crawled upward. She planned to sit at the top and wait. Sooner or later Gertrude would fly by again. Then she would grab hold of Gertrude's tail.

Just as she neared the crest of the roof, Miss Rosemary felt herself slipping. She grabbed for the chimney but missed it. Down, down, down she slid. When she hit the gutter, Miss Rosemary bounced. *Whoosh*. Her dress billowed like a parachute as she sailed through the air and landed in a mass of trumpet vine.

"That crackbrained cow will put me in an early grave," Miss Rosemary moaned as she untangled herself.

Miss Rosemary hobbled to the front porch and sat in her rocking chair. That was her best thinking place. She crossed her arms, set her jaw, and rocked.

And thought.

She rocked and thought without stopping for lunch. She rocked and thought without speaking to the postman. She rocked and thought without answering the phone.

Gertrude, for her part, did not come down. Not once.

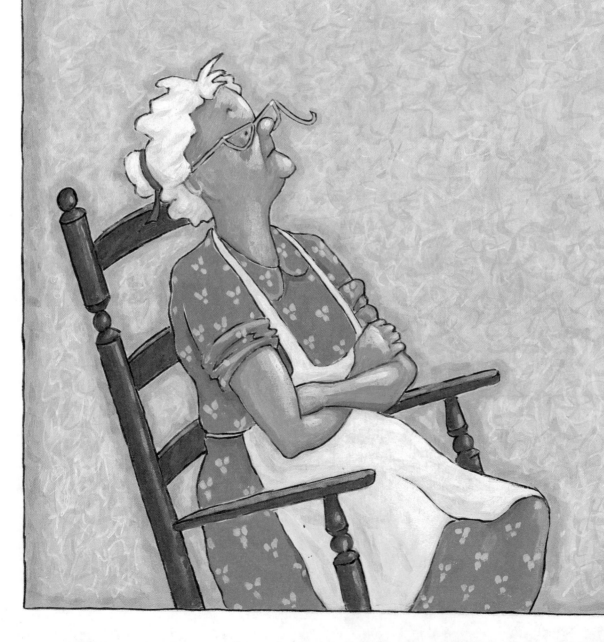

That evening when the sun turned red and the hills turned blue, Miss Rosemary finally had the answer. Wearing a crafty little grin, she rose from her chair and went to the barn. There she got a bucket of paint, a brush, and a large piece of plywood. She made a sign that said,

HELP WANTED.
FULL-TIME COW.
EXPERIENCE DESIRABLE.
APPLY IN PERSON.

Miss Rosemary put the sign on her front gate. She stole an upward glance at Gertrude, who pretended not to be curious.

Then Miss Rosemary went to the attic. She dug
around until she found two pairs of old roller skates.
She took these to her sewing room.

Next she emptied all her boxes of fabric pieces
and made a huge pile in the middle of the floor. She
went through the mound and selected just the right
scraps and squares. The rest, she decided, would do
for stuffing.

Miss Rosemary sat down and began to sew. She
worked all through the night. Her sewing machine
never stopping humming.

Just as the sun cleared the hilltops, out of the house
Miss Rosemary came...
followed by Matilda.

Miss Rosemary pulled Matilda to the barnyard—
right up to Gertrude's feeding bin, which was right
beside Gertrude's salt lick, which was right across
from Gertrude's watering trough.

Miss Rosemary took the bucket of paint and the
brush, and she changed the sign on the front gate.
She put a big *X* through the HELP WANTED part. Then
she added some new words. The sign now said,

HELP WANTED.
FULL TIME COW.
EXPERIENCE DESIRABLE.
APPLY IN PERSON.
NO COWS NEEDED!
POSITION FILLED.

Miss Rosemary went back to Matilda
and gave her a pat on the nose.
"What a perfect cow," she said,
a bit louder than necessary.

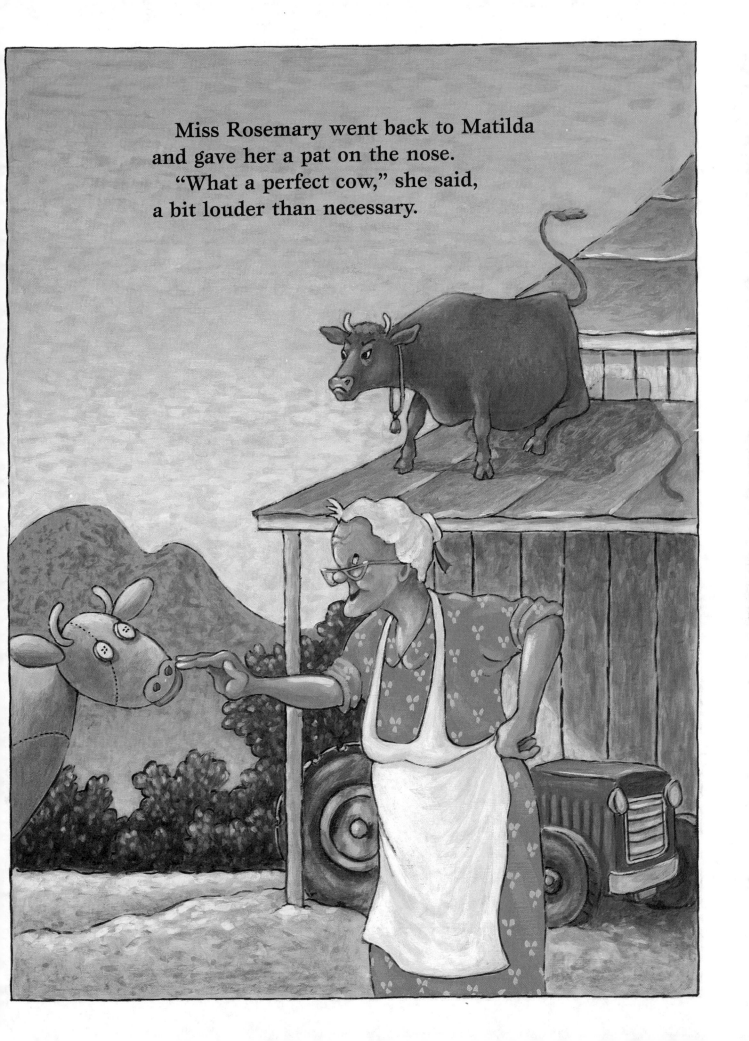

With that, Miss Rosemary went inside, fixed herself a hearty plate of scrambled eggs and toast, and sat down to eat by the window.

Gertrude circled above Matilda, slowly coming closer and closer. Around and around she flew until finally she made a sudden zoom for the clouds. Straight up she climbed. Way up she climbed.

Gertrude came down like a rocket. *Ssssssssss—*
THUNK! She landed squarely on Matilda and
mashed her flat.

Miss Rosemary smiled and finished her
scrambled eggs.

Later Gertrude returned to munching grass and swishing her tail, as cows are supposed to do. Miss Rosemary was relieved. But she couldn't help thinking…it seemed that Gertrude was spending a lot of time around the farm machinery.

"Silly me." Miss Rosemary clucked. "It's a known fact cows don't drive tractors."